WISH ON A
WINTER MOON

ALASKA DJINN SERIES
BOOK 1

K. KIELY

BOREAL SPARKS PRESS, LLC

CONTENTS

1. Rosa   1
2. Djinn   5
3. Rosa   9
4. Djinn   13
5. Rosa   19
6. Ardeth   29
7. Rosa   35
8. Ardeth   41
9. Rosa   51
10. Ardeth   55
11. Rosa   61
12. Rosa   69
13. Ardeth   75
14. Rosa   79
15. Ardeth   83
16. Rosa   87
17. Ardeth   91
18. Rosa   95

Thank you for reading!   97
Author Note   99
Acknowledgments   101
About the author   103

1

ROSA

Things couldn't get any worse than this. And if it could.... Well, I didn't want to think about that.

It was pitch black, freaking cold, and snow had begun to fall. My rundown Toyota had died, stranding me on a mountain not far outside Anchorage. How was I to know that winter would arrive in Southcentral Alaska *in October*? In Arizona, October meant trick-or-treating in shorts. Besides, it'd been warm when I'd arrived in Alaska at the beginning of June. I'd figured I had another month before white stuff started falling from the sky. Rookie mistake—and sadly, not my first.

With my cell phone as deceased as my car, I had no way to call for help. Not that I *had* anyone to call. If I did, maybe I wouldn't be jobless and living in my beater Camry. There wasn't anyone waiting for me back in Phoenix, either.

I sat in the deserted trailhead parking lot where, for the last fifteen minutes, I'd been struggling to start my poor vehicle. There'd been much pleading, definitely some cursing, and perhaps a few frustrated tears. I'd driven up here on a whim, my timing such that the last hikers had left just as

I'd arrived. Did I have a parking pass? Nope. Didn't have the money for it, so yeah. Couldn't get blood from a stone. I'd never really understood that phrase before now.

Maybe I should have huddled in the car to steal whatever warmth was left. Instead, I stood next to my worthless hunk of metal, and stared up into the sky. I'd come up to Mt. Whatever in search of peace, something I needed now more than ever. Thankfully, I had my extra-large coffee from the mini-mart—paid with what meager change I'd found in the cushions of my car seat—to keep me warm. The stars weren't anywhere to be found, shrouded by clouds releasing the first big white flakes of winter, but the moon still shone through the occasional break in cloud cover. It was beautiful, and I wished I could appreciate it more. Hard to do when my hands and nose were turning to ice.

I gazed at the full moon, peeking through the clouds, and tried to find a flicker of hope. All I found was a grumbly tummy, rioting at its near-empty state. I wondered if there were still two granola bars in the glove box, leftover from a road trip three years ago when my life had possessed some semblance of stability. It hadn't been stable for a while now, and I didn't know when it would be again. If ever. But they could help quiet the rumbles and gurgles in my stomach.

I still had a twenty squirreled away in my purse, one I'd been debating using for either food or gas. Right now, gas wasn't the problem, and twenty bucks wouldn't cover the new battery I needed.

Or a better life.

Did I have any tissues in the glove box? Or maybe a stiff, crinkly, fast-food napkin? My nose was going to run if I stayed out here much longer.

I sniffed, trying to convince myself that my snotty nose was due to the chill and not the tears blurring my vision.

That was all I needed—snot and tears freezing to my cheeks. I'd make such an attractive corpse when tomorrow's hikers stumbled across popsicle-me up here.

My current choices were: a) huddle in my car until someone found me, b) hike until I found someone to help, or c) give up. I wanted to do the hike, but not down a mountain in the dark with who knows what kind of critters lurking unseen. Besides, I didn't have the strength, and my feet were already blocks of ice in my worn-out Adidas. Option A was really the same as C but with a smidgen of hope. Not sure I had any of that left.

It sucked that I couldn't at least enjoy the view, but it was too dark to see much from the parking lot. What on earth had I been thinking, coming up here at sunset?

I'd hoped for one final, spectacular memory to hold on to before I checked into the local homeless shelter tonight. As usual, my poor decision-making skills had landed me in more trouble than expected.

I leaned against my car until I remembered how filthy it was, so I pushed away from it. My insides barely warmed with a sip of bitter, burned, sickly sweetened lukewarm coffee. I sniffed again, blinking away the moisture in my eyes, and the moon's edges sharpened. So much ugliness in the city below, but only beauty from this mountaintop. The snow made the faintest shushing noise as it fell on the ground, on my car, on me. I pulled up my hood; damp hair wouldn't help keep me warm.

It was peaceful here, but I'd never felt more alone and hopeless. Tears filled my eyes again, my sobs puffing clouds into the air. Why had I believed that things would get better? What evidence did I have that hope would give me what I needed?

"I wish..." *For security.*

"I wish..." *For comfort.*

"I wish..." *An end to the emptiness.* "Please."

A mist formed, and I squinted. Where had it come from? Not from my breath, I couldn't possibly breathe out that much.

The vapor in front of me gathered like a cloud, and from that mist emerged...a man.

2

DJINN

AH, CALLED AGAIN TO FULFILL THE VAPID WISHES OF SOME poor soul who felt they had not been done right by the world. *Sigh.*

The mist cleared, and before me stood a woman bundled in inadequate garb for the winter weather, eyes wide, mouth agape.

A few moments of conversation would tell me if she were an unintelligent specimen, or if her intellectual talents were only well disguised.

I had to give her credit, however. Rather than drop the cup in her hands, she gripped it tighter, and the dark liquid bubbled up through the hole in the lid.

"Who...what are you?" she squeaked.

My excellent night vision allowed me to see her hazel eyes narrow as she inched back toward the vehicle behind her.

"Where did you come from?" One hand groped for the door handle, as if that hulk of metal could protect her from me.

Not that I wished her harm. My purpose here was quite the opposite.

"I am Djinn," I answered, modulating my voice so that it did not boom out like a foghorn. "You summoned me."

She shook her head, somehow still holding that paper cup, though now it tipped so that coffee dripped into the dusting of snow at her feet. "I did no such thing." The hood on her coat slid back as she continued to shake her head, revealing straight, dark hair that hung past her shoulders. "I wouldn't even know how."

This was always the tedious part, explaining why I'd come. Though some who summoned me were well aware of the process, many times I appeared to those who inadvertently reached out in need. She must be of that ilk, and would require more deft handling than the rest.

I much preferred a straightforward transaction with a knowledgeable mistress.

"Indeed, you *did* summon me. Did you not make a wish?" I asked.

"Uh, no. I didn't." The woman's spine straightened, as did the cup, no longer dripping its contents.

"You surely did, or I would not be here now."

Her nose was red with cold, and her body shivered almost imperceptibly, though I did not think it was due to fear. In the thousand years I had spent in this realm, I had come to understand much about the human race. I was able to determine whether a person was a fighter or a coward, an altruist or a selfish bastard. This one looked to be a fighter at her core, even if she had a sense of hopelessness wrapped around her.

Her wishes would make all of that clear soon enough. Time to forge ahead.

"I am Djinn, and I am here to grant you the customary

three wishes. Shall we begin, or would you rather stand here and freeze to death?" Easy choices were always a good prod for those mired in indecision.

"Three wishes?"

Wonderful. This one was a parrot. Thankfully, I had all the time in the world. "Yes. You are familiar with the tales of djinn who grant wishes, I assume?"

Her face brightened with recognition. "Ohhhhh, a genie!" She whistled, long and low. "What are you doing here? Aren't you a bit far from home?"

Home. As if that were a physical place for my kind. "Do you truly believe that a being with my powers is restricted by the geopolitical boundaries determined by humans?" How insulting.

Full lips pressed together, then she responded, "Good point. Is it also logical to assume that you aren't cold even though you are only half dressed and a bit blue?" She waved a hand toward me.

"I am not cold, and this is my customary appearance." I crossed my arms over my chest. "Are you finished with your inane questions? Shall we proceed?"

"Oh, by all means." There was a haughty tilt to her mouth, and a flash of ire in her eyes. This one had spirit, no matter how quashed it may have been. "Do let us proceed."

"I shall begin with the parameters of our arrangement. No point in having you ask for things that are not available to you."

"Wait a minute. I thought genies granted every wish."

"First, I am Djinn, not a 'genie.' Second, I cannot grant any wish that will either take a life or directly prevent someone from dying. Do not even consider requesting immortality; that boon is not for the likes of you." I looked down my nose at her when I said that last bit. "Wishes may not be used to solve problems on a global scale such as hunger, climate change, or world peace. Nor can they be used to request additional wishes."

"I figured as much," she said. "Anything else?"

"Yes, and listen well." I stared into those hazel eyes, impressing upon her the weight of the consequences of her future choices. "Once I have manifested your final wish, I will no longer be bound to you. I will disappear from your life, never to be seen again." I pushed more power into my voice. "Do you understand?"

"Yes, I understand." She had deepened her voice in mimicry of mine, then followed with a snort. "Are you always this doom and gloom?"

My voice reverted to its usual volume for conversing with humans. "Are you?"

She sobered. "Not usually. But I guess if I were all cheerfulness and light, you wouldn't be here." Under her breath, she muttered, "If he's even here. He probably isn't. I'm just going insane or something."

I could not ignore those words. "Make your first request. If I am real, you will receive what you want. If I am not, you may at least receive a welcome illusion."

3

ROSA

I HAD MYSELF A REAL-LIFE GENIE AT MY BECK AND CALL. Either that, or a hypothermic hallucination.

And I had an excellent imagination, if I said so myself. He must have stood nearly seven feet tall, bare-chested and well-muscled, his skin a pale dusky blue. He wore loose-fitted pants and flimsy shoes not suitable for the chilly Alaskan weather. Frankly, he looked more hypothermic than me. But his face—whew! It made me hot and molten inside. He reminded me of that guy from *The Mummy* franchise. Not Brendan Fraser, but Mr. Hottie with the shoulder-length black hair, flashing dark eyes, and sinful mouth.

Meaning I was definitely hallucinating. Good to know.

I stomped my feet, hoping they wouldn't shatter like ice cubes. "I suppose anything is better than just standing here and freezing to death. Okay, I'll play along. But first, I'm Rosa." I thrust out my frozen hand, wondering if his would be just as cold, or if he would deign to touch mine. "What should I call you? Do you have an actual name?"

His eyes dropped to my hand, no other part of him moving. I could sense the disdain from here, and no amount of delusion would convince me otherwise. He didn't shake my hand, but he did say, "You may call me Djinn."

Alrighty then. For a figment of my imagination, this was not going well.

Back to wish number one. "I want a home. Wait, not yet!" Just in case I wasn't hallucinating—ha!—I should probably make sure I covered all the bases. "How specific do I need to be? I mean, should I say that it needs to be in a good neighborhood, not out in the boonies where I'm miles away from the nearest grocery store?"

Mr. Hottie gave me a bored-yet-supercilious look before answering. "Be as specific as you like. Any alteration after the wish is granted will be considered an additional wish."

I probably should have read all of the fine print first. But I was a fast learner.

"Don't go granting this wish until I get it all out, alright?" I waited, until he finally nodded. Clearing my throat, I started from scratch. "I want a house that is all mine and that no one can ever take away from me. It doesn't have to be really big or anything, I'm not looking for a mansion. I just need enough space that I don't feel cramped. I want it fully furnished, with all the necessities included. There should be a view of the mountains." I'd rather look at the mountains from in front of a roaring fire than be trapped in the cold on top of one any day. "And a yard where I can plant things, and maybe have space for a dog to run around. Oh, and like I said, in a nice neighborhood. I'd like some friendly neighbors, if that's possible."

He looked at me, face impassive, saying nothing.

"I think that's it," I said, rocking back on my frozen heels.

"You think, or you know?"

"Yes, that's all for the first wish." God, I was going to feel so stupid when I finally returned to reality and found myself talking to no one.

"So be it." There was a depth and power to his voice as he spoke those words, something extra that hadn't been present before. And then—

I swear, I blinked once and suddenly found myself in a residential neighborhood with wide streets, sidewalks, and yards with meticulously pruned hedges. I stood in front of a house that was nicer than anything I'd ever lived in, or even visited before. My car was parked in the driveway in front of it. How... No, don't ask. Just go along for the ride. It was such a *good* ride. The best ever.

"Is...is this *my* house?" I couldn't see the genie, but I could feel him at my back. Not touching me, but definitely near. "It's so big!"

He huffed out what might have been a laugh, if he ever did that sort of thing. It was my dream, my delusion. Of course, he would laugh. "Open the door."

Now it was my turn to chuckle. "Shouldn't that be 'Open, sesame'?" I glanced back at him. His muscular arms rested across his chest, and he glowered at me. "Fine. Not like it was a good joke, anyway."

"No, it was not."

But he'd responded, so I counted that as a win.

I marched up to the front door. Hopefully, this wouldn't backfire on me. Lights blazed from the windows. If this place belonged to someone else, I was going to be horribly embarrassed and likely arrested for home invasion. But my car was in the driveway, right? How could that be when it wasn't even running?

Taking a deep breath, I put my hand on the doorknob and turned it. The door swung open, and warmth washed over my icy face and hands as I stepped into the foyer.

"Hello?" I called out, praying no one would answer.

"What are you doing?" Mr. Hottie stood beside me, a crease between his fine brows.

"Checking to see if anyone is home." *Duh.*

"Who would be here? It's *your* home. It belongs to no one else. Exactly as you requested."

I stood on frozen tiptoes as though that would give me a better look past the foyer. "It looks lived in. You didn't boot anyone out of their home for me, did you?"

Maybe he could have looked more insulted, but I couldn't see how. "Certainly not!"

He seemed even larger standing in the foyer of my new home than he had on that mountain. I peered up at him. "This is really mine? Like, for real and for always? No one is going to come and throw me out or arrest me or anything?"

"No. This is your home, the one you wished for. It is entirely yours for as long as you choose." His face was grave, and I wanted so much to believe him.

Wishes were choices, and I had so many inside me. In that moment, I chose to believe.

4

DJINN

THE YOUNG WOMAN APPEARED SLOW TO UNDERSTAND THE situation at times, but perhaps it was naïveté and disbelief instead. She had thought to ask for what she wanted in a way that ensured it would not be taken from her. That demonstrated foresight I had not expected.

I also did not expect her to throw herself into my arms, embracing me in thanks. Or, rather, into my chest as she was petite. I have encountered various demonstrations of gratitude over the centuries, and have learned to tolerate them reasonably well. But this instance startled me, and I found myself holding her against me. The warmth inside the dwelling caused her scent to rise up, tickling my nose.

It was not entirely pleasant, the odor of unwashed clothing mixed with rancid coffee, but it was nothing that a long bath, laundry, and hygiene could not mend. In spite of this, holding her was both comforting and alluring. A strange thought, that. And not as unwelcome as it ought to be.

Attempting to be gentle, I grasped her shoulders and firmly pushed her away. I immediately ached for her touch.

Two wishes remained. I only hoped she dispatched them quickly as most do, thereby releasing me from my obligation before I succumbed to these troublesome desires. My long years of experience had taught me that forming an attachment to a mistress was ill-advised at best.

"Go." The order came out harsh, a bark, and her eyes reflected the hurt I had inflicted. The ache would be fleeting; still, I softened my voice. "Explore your new home."

A grin split Rosa's face, and she took a few quick steps before stopping short. "Oops! Boots off. House rule." She peeked over her shoulder at me, glancing at my feet. "I guess you don't have to, though. Do you even have snow on your slippers?"

I huffed.

"Fine," she said. "You can keep yours on." She bent, unlacing her boots, her ample bottom peeking out from under her jacket.

I shouldn't be noticing her bottom. Or her anything.

The hood slid back as Rosa removed her coat, and the unusual color of her hair froze me in my place. It was the darkest shade of red imaginable, almost black but with a fire burning deep within.

This fanciful train of thought was very unlike me. It raced through me, dangerous and thrilling.

"Is there a—oh, perfect!" Rosa opened the closet and hung up her jacket. "All neat and tidy."

She was practically bouncing on her toes. I crossed my arms over my chest before she could fling herself at me again.

"Go on. Look around." I inclined my head toward the room to the right.

Quivering with excitement, Rosa looked right, then left.

The door to the left was closed while the entrance to the room on the right had no door. "What's in there?"

"The library."

"Seriously?" Her eyes were huge in her face, wonder giving her face an innocent quality.

I nodded.

Rosa dragged her bottom lip through her teeth as she gazed at the closed library door. "I'm going to save that one for the end."

I felt sure she must also save the best morsel for last. Did she choose to prolong and savor every pleasurable experience?

Turning to the right, Rosa gingerly entered a formal living area, chairs and a sofa arranged around a fireplace. She traced the mantel with fingers still pale from the cold.

With hardly a thought, I lit a fire in the hearth. She should be warm in her new home.

"Ohhhh," she breathed, rubbing her hands together in front of the flames.

She was whispering to herself, and I stepped closer to hear.

"Don't wake up. Don't wake up."

She believed she was dreaming. That I was not real, nor was her new home.

This happened with some frequency, particularly in instances where the summoning was not intentional. But her disbelief made my chest tighten in a way I did not understand.

Rosa continued through the room, touching the furniture, even the walls as she passed. Her eyes were wide, taking in every detail, like a child encountering some exciting and unexpected delight. The difference between the despair in her eyes when I first appeared and now was remarkable.

This was what made my task bearable. One of the few things that made it so.

All the centuries that I had been bound to this work had made me cynical, jaded, and distrustful of humans. By and large, they were greedy, selfish creatures, only grasping for that which would raise themselves up while dashing anyone else to the rocks below. Rarely did I encounter someone who wanted only what was necessary and nothing more. Rosa could yet prove me wrong, but my instincts told me that she would not abuse this privilege. Her second wish would reveal more.

Her stockinged feet padded quietly on the thick carpet through the dining room, shushing along the hardwood floor in the hall to the kitchen in the back of the house. She stopped short, just inside the doorway, and I longed to see her face when a gasp escaped her lips.

"Oh my god." She clasped her hands in front of her, as though suddenly afraid to touch anything for fear it would disappear. "This is mine?"

I had thought it a rhetorical question until she glanced back at me. I nodded, the tears welling in her eyes stealing my voice.

What was happening to me? I could not recall experiencing a fascination so strong, certainly not with a human.

I needed space.

No longer bouncing along but slowly gliding from the granite countertop to the stainless steel gas range to the cherrywood cabinets, Rosa reverently caressed it all. She halted at the sink, staring out the window into the darkness. "I hope there's a view. Maybe a place to hang a bird feeder."

Then she spun on her toes, slid to the refrigerator, and

whipped it open. "Yes!" She pumped her fist into the air, then grabbed a container of strawberry yogurt. "Do you want something to eat?"

"No."

"Don't you get hungry?" She didn't look up, searching for a spoon in the drawers.

"Not as such."

Her brows came together in puzzlement. "Huh?"

"I may partake of food and drink, but I do not require it."

"Oh." She paused long enough to eat a spoonful of yogurt. "Well, I love to cook for people. And to eat."

I could appreciate that. The relish with which Rosa devoured the yogurt hinted that she may not have had adequate food recently. In spite of that, she was well cushioned, plush and rounded from her bosom to her hips and thighs. Only her hair and her nose created straight lines.

She scraped the last bit of yogurt from the container, and licked every trace from the spoon.

I couldn't wrest my gaze from her mouth.

A problematic situation, at best. Disastrous, at worst. Being near Rosa heightened all my senses, threatening to destroy my good judgment.

I took several steps back, distancing myself from her.

Rosa turned from discarding the yogurt container in the trash. "What's wrong? Do I reek?" She sniffed her sweater, then huffed against her palm. "I do, don't I? This is mortifying." She cringed, pressing her back against the counter. "I'm sorry. I haven't been able to do laundry for a while."

She smelled no worse than someone who had traveled far, but could not have looked more ashamed.

"No, you do not reek. I merely wanted to give you space to enjoy your new home." I could not reveal the true reason for my reserve, and give her ideas of how to potentially manipulate me. I had encountered humans with hidden agendas before.

"Thank you, even if that's not the whole truth." Her body relaxed, but she maintained the distance I'd placed between us.

A blessing, and what I needed if not what I desired.

"Shall we continue the tour?" The sooner we concluded this stage, the sooner she could indulge in her second wish. I swept an arm toward the hall. "After you, mistress."

5

ROSA

Ugh. I'm sure Djinn was just being kind, saying I didn't stink. I hadn't been able to do laundry properly for a month, and had only been able to take sponge baths in public restrooms. My deodorant wasn't *that* effective.

I led the way back down the hall to the stairs, hoping he stayed far enough behind that he couldn't smell me. I was desperate for a shower and clean clothes, but first, I needed to see the rest of this gorgeous house.

Was it really all mine, forever and ever? Hard to imagine, even harder to believe. Honestly, I didn't know if I believed it yet, or what it would mean if I did. If this was a hypothermic delusion, would it just get better and better until I faded out? There were much worse ways to go. I should probably care more, but I was determined to enjoy what was in front of me for as long as it lasted.

Both the house and the man. Genie. Djinn.

At the top of the stairs, I turned to the left and entered a large, open room, already set up for my crafts: space for my sewing machine, a cutting table, for designing needlework patterns and making my book art. I could spread out and not have to pack everything up after each creative session. I'd never been so glad to have saved my sewing machine and craft tools, now crammed into the front passenger footwell of my car.

"How...?" I scrambled for words. "How could you know —" My hand flapped in the air like a drunken bat, gesturing at the craft paradise before me.

"Would you like to see the rest of the upstairs?" Djinn asked.

He didn't address my feeble question, but I caught the mischievous glint in his eyes. Maybe the rest of the tour would provide the answer.

I nodded, struck anew by the height and breadth of him. He dwarfed the doorway, and ducked as he passed through it. For the first time, I got a good look at him from behind: well-muscled back narrowing to his waist, and what appeared to be a gorgeous ass covered by loose silk trousers. I couldn't tell anything about his legs, but I was sure they were equally spectacular. And the same light dusky blue as the skin of his torso.

Stop perving on the genie. Things I never thought I'd tell myself. Par for the course for this nutty day.

Djinn flung open the double doors to the master suite— I had a master suite!—to reveal a king-size, four-poster bed against a wall, and a sofa in front of the fireplace at the other end of the room. The colors were my favorite, rich jewel tones that radiated warmth. That bed looked so comfy, and I wanted to fall onto it and sleep for a week.

"You can lie down," Djinn said. "It's yours, after all."

Okay, that was spooky. How did he know what I was thinking?

He didn't have to tell me twice.

With a whoop, I flung myself backward onto the center

of the bed. It responded with a little bounce before I settled softly into the down comforter spread across its surface.

"Ahhh!" This was heaven. And to think that I'd be sleeping here tonight, in this bed. All alone...

My eyes strayed to the imposing figure in the doorway.

Nope. Not entertaining that thought. It was ridiculously inappropriate. And far too intriguing.

"I don't want to get up," I whined, rolling myself off the edge of the bed and onto my feet. I didn't linger in my present state of less than freshness.

"There is no need," Djinn said. "You may stay in bed as long as you like."

Oh, dude, don't tempt me! Hearing those words in his voice made me want more than a good night's sleep.

"I'm already up, so I might as well keep looking." I gave the pillow a longing pat as I headed for what must be a closet. And what a closet it was. Walk-in, of course, with drawers and rods along both walls. Even a padded bench to sit on while dressing.

And it was filled with clothes.

A giggle bubbled out of my mouth. This was seriously the best delusion ever.

"Why are you laughing?" Djinn asked, giving me a concerned look. As well he should.

I ran a hand along a row of hangers. "I can't imagine ever being able to wear all of these. How do I know if they're even my size?"

"They are perfectly fitted to you. But if they do not suit you, you may request different garments. An entirely new wardrobe, if you like. All you need to do is ask, and it will be yours, mistress." His gaze had sharpened, and I had the impression that he wanted me to make my second wish already.

"I'm not your mistress. Call me Rosa." I might not be able to change the nature of our temporary arrangement, but we didn't have to be formal about it.

"You *are* my mistress for as long as I am bound to you." He inclined his head, though there was nothing subservient about the gesture. "But I will call you by your name, if you prefer."

It must be awful, being shackled to someone else for the duration of the wish-granting process. How much control did he have over his existence? Would he even tell me if I asked? That seemed too serious a topic for the moment, but I definitely wanted to come back to it.

"I do prefer, thanks." I exited the closet and we moved over to the sitting area near the fireplace. The door next to it probably led to the master bathroom. "I feel like I should call you something other than Djinn, though. I mean, it's kind of like calling a dog 'dog,' right?"

His face went all haughty, as if I'd insulted him. "Are you equating djinn with a dog?"

"No, of course not!" I raised my hands in defense. "I would never. I just mean it's like naming something after what it is. It seems very unimaginative and kind of demeaning."

Djinn huffed through his nose. "Demeaning? I should say so, comparing me to a dog."

"Really, I didn't mean it like that. I'm sorry I offended you."

I laid a hand on his arm, startled by how warm he was to the touch. With his cool hue, I'd imagined he'd be cold. When I'd hugged him in the foyer, I'd still been bundled up, my skin separated from his by my jacket.

And now I was thinking about skin against skin.

I tugged the cuffs of my sleeves over my fingers. "I'd

rather call you by your name, not just what you are. If that's fine by you."

"You may call me Djinn, for that is what I am called."

"But is that *actually* your name, or just what people call you because they don't know any better?"

"Does it matter?"

"It matters to me."

"Why should it matter what you call me?"

"Because names are special. I read something in a book once." I sat down on the sofa, suddenly weary of being on my feet. "It was about names having power. You're very powerful, and it seems insulting that you don't have a name of your own, one not shared by anyone else."

His eyes shuttered, and his arms crossed protectively over his chest. "Assuming that assertion is correct, why would I ever give you my name and thus power over me?"

Oh. Yeah, he had a point.

"I get it now." I leaned forward, elbows on my knees, staring into the fireplace. When did he light the fire in this room? I must have missed that. "Do you mind if I choose a name to call you instead? It wouldn't be your true name—I won't ask you to tell me—but I won't have to call you Djinn either."

He hummed thoughtfully, rocking back on his heels. "I suppose that would be acceptable. But no silly or disrespectful names. That I will not abide."

"Certainly not." I rose, gazing up into his stern face with its dark eyes and sharp features. "I'll call you Ardeth." I hoped he wouldn't ask where I came up with it. Explaining about the hottie in *The Mummy* would make me blush horribly.

"Ardeth." He repeated it slowly, as if tasting each sound,

then nodded. "That is tolerable enough. You may call me Ardeth, if you wish."

Yeah, I saw what he did there, but I wasn't falling for it.

"I would like that very much, but not as a wish." *I'm not as naive as I look, buddy.*

"Noted." The corner of his mouth curled up. "Shall we continue?"

"Indeed, we shall," I said, mimicking his more stilted style of speech. It sounded better coming from him, but he could use some loosening up, and I could use a little fun.

Ardeth followed me into the master bathroom, which was full of every bath item I could have imagined, and was easily the size of the apartment I'd lived in previously. I tried not to think of how much time and effort it would take to keep this house clean, even if it were only me living here. It seemed ungrateful to be concerned about that, but I wasn't going to waste a wish on a housekeeper or cleaning service. That was a luxury I wasn't ready for. Besides, I had something else in mind for Wish Numero Dos.

There were three other bedrooms, another full bathroom down the hall, and a laundry room that had me convinced I might enjoy washing clothes now. No, not really. But it wouldn't be the onerous chore it had once been, either. It was fully stocked with the brands I usually bought, and I made a mental note to put in a load as soon as I could.

But first, I wanted to go explore my library. *My. Library! Holy shit!*

I tried to stay cool as we made our way back downstairs, but my insides were rioting at the thought that I had a real freaking library of my own. When I'd lost basically everything in the past month, the only comfort that hadn't been yanked from me was the public library. It had become my sanctuary. To know that I had my very own treasure trove of reading material felt like the greatest extravagance I could imagine.

Ardeth opened the door for me, a secret smile gracing his striking face, as though he knew what this meant to me. I suppose he did. Entering the cozy room, I stopped a few feet inside the doorway to take it all in. The floor-to-ceiling bookshelves with the obligatory ladder to reach the higher ones. The gorgeous desk—mahogany, I guessed. The wing-back chairs and comfy sofa with a low table between them. The fireplace, lit and the fire crackling, just like in the living room and master bedroom. How many fireplaces did this place have? Then there were the windows, as large as I could have hoped for. In the dark, I had no idea what the view was like beyond, but I imagined it would be spectac-ular like everything else I'd seen so far. That had been part of my wish, after all.

And the books. More than I'd ever seen anywhere outside of a school or public library, and they were mine.

I started with the shelves directly across from the door-way, tracing the spines as I read the titles. It only took a few moments to realize—

"These are my...." I turned to Ardeth, unable to finish.

"Your favorite tales, yes," he confirmed.

Not only my favorites that I'd read, but also many I'd been meaning to read, even the secret books and graphic novels I'd never mentioned to a soul.

"But how could you know?" I demanded, pointing at the shelves.

He gave me that haughty eyebrow.

"Can you read my mind?"

"No, I cannot. But any personal details directly related to

a wish are perfectly reflected in the results regardless of any knowledge I may or may not have."

Whew! Because no way did I need him to know how he affected me. Dealing with the abundance of my first wish was overwhelming enough. Any acknowledgment of my attraction to him would probably make me faint.

And a more pressing issue needed to be addressed.

"Ardeth. This, all of this, everything... It's so much. I never dreamed of a library, or a big kitchen, or a craft room." I gulped down air, fighting back tears. "I don't deserve it."

His gaze was thoughtful, but not necessarily kind. Sharp, and a bit suspicious. "Why do you say that?"

"Because this is more than I need. I'm not as bad off as many other people out there. I hadn't even checked into the homeless shelter yet. But there are families with young children, teens who've been kicked out of their homes, who need this more than I do." Guilt settled onto my shoulders, making me slump with the weight. "It's not fair. I got myself into this predicament with my lousy judgment and poor choices. What did I do to deserve all of this?"

Ardeth crossed his arms over his muscular slab of a chest, eyes dark and unreadable. "You did nothing to deserve it. You made a wish. Wishes are not to be mistaken for a reward, any more than misfortune or unforeseen hardship might be construed as punishment. If you are unhappy with the results of your first wish, you may correct it with your second or third. Only be certain to craft them with care so that you do not end with more regrets than you started with."

As I worked through his words, the following silence stretched between us, broken only by the crackling of the fire.

They were harsh, the points he'd made. I wasn't special. I hadn't earned this opportunity to turn my life around in such a fantastic style. But I wasn't powerless, either.

That gave me hope. And hope gave me a wisp of an idea.

6

ARDETH

I needed Rosa to declare her remaining wishes quickly. Being bound to this woman was causing me to have...feelings. Feelings for her. Feelings that inspired the urge to aid her beyond the boundaries I had long since set for these transactions, and which I masked with rough truths intended to bruise her soft heart.

Instead, my words only seemed to steel her spine. I could not help but admire her. That would never do.

There must be a way to convince her to reveal her wishes soon.

Once Rosa had seen her fill of the library, she excused herself to shower and change into fresh garments. I could hear her singing enthusiastically off-key from the master bathroom as I stood in the hall like the idiot I was.

For some reason, I found her singing charming, but I was in no mood to be charmed. Yet I could not stop myself from smiling, even so.

This was dangerous. If she smelled enticing when wearing odiferous rags, how much more powerful would the effect be once she was freshly bathed?

I forced myself to retreat to the kitchen, assuming Rosa's next step would be to fill her belly. The small container of yogurt could not possibly have sated her after going hungry as she had. The urge to wave my hand and produce a cooked meal, ready and waiting for her, was strong enough to grit my teeth against. The more nonobligatory magic I performed in her service, the more closely I would bind myself to her.

Rosa practically skipped down the hall to the kitchen, and my jaw clenched while my groin tightened. She was wearing no more than shorts and a light top with narrow straps. It may not have been intended as provocative, but it set my body aflame. Her ample breasts pressed against the thin fabric, and her plush thighs were on full display.

The thought of my fingertips denting her flesh as I pressed those thighs wide caused my shaft to stiffen and throb. Then a waft of roses invaded my nostrils as she stopped within arm's reach.

"I feel *so* much better!" she chirped. "But now I could eat a horse. Or I could if I weren't a vegetarian. Let's see what we've got to eat around here."

At least she did not require a response from me. I feared nothing intelligible would come from my mouth.

As Rosa bent to peer into the refrigerator, I had to turn my back. It hardly helped, and did nothing to keep my imagination from running amok. I must have growled my frustration.

"Ardeth? Everything okay over there?" she asked. "I thought you said you weren't hungry."

"That is correct," I snapped.

"I thought I heard your stomach rumble." She continued to rummage through the kitchen, and I heard her pull items out of the pantry. "Are you sure I can't tempt you to join me?"

Rosa absolutely tempted me. I might not be hungering for food, but I definitely hungered in a way I had not in all my years.

I was no stranger to the delights of the flesh. I had both given and received sexual pleasure before, but never had I felt so compelled by a human woman, as though I had been ensorcelled.

Could Rosa be a genuine sorceress, feigning rough circumstances to gain my sympathy? Had she enthralled me? Unlikely, but she certainly had some hold over me.

The clank of a pan on the stovetop was followed by the sound of eggs cracking and Rosa whipping them in a bowl. I peeked over my shoulder, grateful she was no longer bent over.

Unfortunately, her current position was no better. The motion of the fork in the bowl caused Rosa's breasts to sway beneath their thin covering, and her hips followed suit. It was like an erotic dance, sinful yet completely innocent at the same time. Her focus rested entirely on the food, and she paid me no mind as she slipped the beaten eggs into the pan with a sizzle of butter.

My mouth watered.

"Perhaps...." I halted, and Rosa's eyes met mine expectantly. "Perhaps I could join you in a meal."

Her smile blinded me. How could such a small thing feel like I had given her a tremendous gift? It made no sense whatsoever.

"I'd like that." Rosa's voice was as soft as her eyes. "Very much." Then she turned back to the stove.

It was inconceivable how Rosa managed to both eat and

talk with equal eagerness, and yet not speak with her mouth full. She was delightful company; I did not know why I was surprised by that discovery. And she was also adept at turning simple ingredients into a delicious repast. The eggs and buttered toast were tastier than any lavish meal I had eaten.

"Thank you for joining me, Ardeth." Rosa paused from tidying the kitchen. I wanted to help, but could not risk being so close to her. "I would have felt awkward eating in front of you, and I really wanted your company."

"You are a good cook." I could give her that tiny bit of praise without allowing her to know how she affected me. "Is that something you would like to do professionally?"

Rosa's laugh lit me up, my eyes lifting to hers. "No, not really. I just do it for fun. I bake, mostly."

"Rosa." Did it sound as reverent in her ears as it tasted on my tongue? Names had power, indeed. "Have you chosen your second wish yet?"

She leaned her back against the kitchen counter, crossing her arms over her chest. "I'm not sure yet how I want to ask it. I need to think it over tonight. I'll tell you tomorrow, okay?"

A canny approach from such a young woman. She was intelligent and deliberate. A formidable foe, if that was what she was. She would be an equally formidable partner.

But not mine.

I could never have a partner in this realm. At best, I had an agreeable mistress for a limited time. This was my life, my existence, and it would continue for countless years more.

A sudden emptiness carved itself out of my chest, gaping, echoing. For once, I longed for more than my freedom. I yearned for belonging, for a binding of the heart and soul, not only of the will that was rarely my own. And I wished...

I wished to be bound to Rosa. To be chosen by her, desired by her, loved by her. A dizzying and improbable realization, and a precipitous one.

"Yes, tomorrow." I shifted my feet, restless to move. "You should rest. Sleep deeply and well. We will speak in the morning."

Rosa retreated to her room while I silently prowled the hallway outside. I should have remained downstairs in the library, or settled into one of the spare bedrooms she had offered for my use. But I had both energy to burn and a need to stay close.

The only way out of this situation was for her to complete her wishes so I could move on. If only that were what I truly desired.

I had heard tales of djinn who had been irrevocably drawn to a master or mistress by an attraction wholly unrelated to the binding of the wish. But I had never personally known any of my brethren to have fallen to this particular fate. The majority had families amongst our own kind. I was an exception in that respect.

My pacing ceased as my thoughts whirled, and I found myself planted outside her bedroom door as a low moan came from inside. It did not sound like a moan of pain, but rather—

Oh. Oh, no.

There was no logical explanation for why my hearing should suddenly become sharper than it had ever been, so acute that I could have been hovering over her body, catching each sigh, every moan as it left her lips. And yet the very atoms of my body were primed to respond to Rosa even as I stood, quivering with iron restraint, outside her door.

I could not possibly hear the slick sound of her fingers sliding through her wet folds, not from here. I could not match the beats of my pounding heart to her sawing breaths. I could not detect the rising scent of the warm musk of her arousal. But it was as real as if I were touching her myself, tracing the curve of her belly with my mouth, the satiny skin of her thighs with my fingertips.

My hand clutched the doorknob, knuckles white with the effort of resisting.

"Ah, Ardeth!" Rosa's strangled cry shot straight through me, and I only barely restrained myself from wrenching open the door and seeing for myself the ecstasy etched on her beautiful face. I pressed my forehead to the cool wood of the door, concentrating until I finally released my grip on the doorknob.

Silently, I moved down the hall and descended the stairs to the library. It was the farthest from her I could be while remaining in this house. I would sleep on the sofa there, not risking the closer proximity of one of the other bedrooms.

My erection was hard as steel; there was no way it would flag without stroking myself to a much-needed climax of my own. Better she not know I had stood witness to her orgasm. Sorceress or not, she had enough power over me already.

7

ROSA

MORNING CAME, OR AT LEAST I ASSUMED IT WAS STILL morning. Daylight, anyway. I had no idea how long I'd slept.

I stretched my arms over my head, wondering at the fact that I no longer questioned the reality of my situation. Had I given in to the delusion entirely, or just accepted that magical things could really happen? Maybe it didn't matter which.

I took a leisurely shower even though I'd taken one the night before. Hot water in abundance was an indulgence I would never take for granted again. When I finished, I spent a little extra time on my hair. I'd combed it back, still damp, the previous night, anxious to get downstairs to fill my rumbling belly. My hair was my best feature, thick and a shade of red so dark that most people believed it couldn't be natural. I'd long since stopped trying to convince anyone otherwise.

A quick survey of my closet produced a soft gray sweater and jeans that somehow fit perfectly.

Somehow. Yeah, I knew how, kinda sorta.

I didn't know where Ardeth was, but I hoped he'd turn

up once I started putting breakfast together. I wanted to feed him again. Was that weird? Probably. He was taking such good care of me, and I wanted to care for him in some small way. Show my gratitude, I guess.

I felt more than gratitude. I felt...so many things.

My plan for today, as far as I had one, was to ask for my second wish. I wanted to be careful about how I submitted my request, covering all the bases. It was more important than ever that I get it right, that I didn't mess it up. This wish really mattered.

When I got downstairs, Ardeth was in the family room, gazing out at the snowy backyard. He didn't look at me when I joined him at the window. "Good morning."

I felt his eyes on me as I assessed the snowfall for myself. "Good morning," he replied. "Did you sleep well?"

I couldn't help a smile. The bed—*my* bed—was the most comfortable surface I'd ever slept on. And to sleep the night through without fear or cold or hunger? Pure bliss. And even more so as I'd imagined his hands on me, his mouth...

Good thing he didn't know about that, or I'd be too embarrassed to face him.

Clearing my throat, I finally answered him. "I did, thanks. How about you? Where did you end up sleeping?"

It seemed unlikely, but I thought I saw him flush, which was the oddest thing given his cool blue skin tone.

Ardeth's voice was a touch raspy, not the smooth silkiness he usually had. "I require little sleep. I stayed in the library."

Okay. If I hadn't been so tired, I might have done the same thing.

"Well, I'm going to make breakfast." I turned toward the kitchen, mentally going through the ingredients I'd found the previous night. "How do you like your pancakes?"

He moved to stand on the opposite side of the kitchen island while I rummaged through the pantry. "As I have never eaten pancakes, I cannot say."

"Well, you're in for a treat because I make damn good ones." I started the griddle preheating on the stovetop. "And get ready for coffee, too." Wait, uh.... "Do you have any food allergies?" No, probably not. "Or, like, dietary restrictions I should know about?"

"None that you need to manage." Ardeth pulled out a stool and sat at the counter. "The food you have here suits me well."

One less hurdle to manage, I guess.

After breakfast, we lingered over coffee—I needed it more than liked it, to be honest. Ardeth relished each sip, and I thought about my next step. The one that didn't involve using a wish.

"So, I still need to find a job." I traced the edge of my mug with my finger. "I have a very nice roof over my head. But I have utilities to pay, and property taxes, and upkeep, and—"

Shaking his head, Ardeth interrupted. "No. When you wished for a home that was secure and yours for the rest of your life, it included those elements as well. Otherwise, it could be taken from you, or you could be penalized or made very uncomfortable if unable to provide payment. Correct?"

Wow. He'd really thought of everything. "I...thank you, Ardeth." Even with a safety net, I needed to put food on the table. And in the back of my mind, I didn't entirely trust that all the details were covered. I would find myself a job, of course, but at least I could take care of my second request before I started my employment search.

Which brought me to the next item on my to-do list. "Then I'm ready for my next wish."

He drew himself up, alert, all relaxation gone. "And that would be?"

"You seem anxious for me to get on with it."

And away from me. *Ouch.*

"Of course," Ardeth replied. "The sooner you state your requests, the sooner I will be released."

Like a punch to the gut, I was reminded of his tether to me, and his lack of choice in the matter. I owed it to him to be quick and efficient with my business.

We were about to get one step closer to the end of his assignment here. Yet I also wanted to understand what his life was like, what he would choose for himself if he could.

That was none of my beeswax, though I was sure he'd phrase it differently.

Back to the task at hand. "Okay, let me explain everything for this next wish. Maybe you can help me do this the right way."

"Certainly," he drawled, leaning back as if he had all day. I had no intention of prolonging his discomfort any longer than necessary.

Deep breath, Rosa.

"When we met, I was in a bad way. More than just stranded on a mountain. I told you some of this last night." Shoving my hands under my thighs to still my restless fingers, I listened to his measured breaths and the ticking of the clock on the wall, the one with the cat's tail swinging back and forth. He waited, giving me space to get the words out.

With a sigh, I met his calm gaze. "If not for you, I would still be in dire straits. And out of hope. I want to do something for people who aren't as lucky as I am. Can I do that with my wish?"

Ardeth tapped the side of his nose with a long, elegant

finger. "Let me see if I have this correct. You intend to use this wish to help those less fortunate than you."

"Uh huh. But I'm not sure the best way to go about it. I need you to help me. I don't want to screw this up." Nobody could mess things up better than I could.

"I regret to say that I cannot aid you in formulating your plan. And as I believe I said before, you cannot end poverty in the world."

"Damn." Slumping in my chair, I fought the urge to give up. I didn't want to be a quitter, not with this.

"Listen carefully, Rosa." I blinked at hearing my name on his lips. It would never stop sounding like pure sex. "I cannot tell you what to wish for, how to phrase your request, or what pitfalls to beware of. But I can wait until you are absolutely sure you have covered every eventuality you can imagine before granting it."

"Can you answer direct questions about your limitations?"

"Many of them, yes."

"Will you listen while I talk it out? You don't have to comment or anything."

"I will," he said solemnly.

The calm authority in his agreement made me believe that I could trust him, that he would find a way to keep me from screwing this up.

He made me think that I could do something good for a change. And if that was a possibility, what other miracles could I imagine?

8

ARDETH

After a methodical and tense strategy session during which I remained technically silent while willing her to read my eyes, I granted Rosa's second wish: to provide resources–food, bedding, money for paying staff, and many other things–to the shelter she had intended to enter the previous evening.

Never had I felt so invested in the details of a wish. Countless transactions, a myriad of forced partnerships, and not one had engaged my emotions as Rosa did.

Her endeavors intrigued me while the woman herself captured my imagination and made me ache and tremble. I had never been so powerless in the presence of a human. I resented this hold she had on me almost as much as I wanted it to continue.

But Rosa had only one wish remaining before I would be called back to my realm.

On the day after her second wish, Rosa ventured to the homeless shelter to see what changes, if any, her wish had wrought. I accompanied her, though not in a form any but she would detect, as she inquired about volunteering, asking numerous questions about the shelter's needs. At the tour's conclusion, she appeared so pleased with all she had learned that, upon our exit, she kissed my cheek in gratitude.

I may have pressed my hand to my cheek.

The following several days passed with little effort on my part beyond making endless pots of tea that we shared in the library as she searched for employment on the computer, or in Rosa's craft room where she whiled away her afternoons. Normally, I would have removed myself from her presence until she was ready to present her final request. Instead, I found myself lingering wherever she went, a shadow haunting her days and being haunted by her, in turn, at night.

Evenings were spent by the fire, either in the library or in the living room, talking and enjoying each other's company. We spoke of many things, most topics inconsequential to my mind, but the most important was what was not said.

Neither of us addressed our mutual reluctance to conclude our business together.

And so our days proceeded, the only alteration being the part-time employment that Rosa obtained at the local public library.

Rosa had confided, however, that she yearned to one day support herself with her artwork. She marveled that she had been provided all the needed supplies and tools. The spacious room upstairs had indeed been transformed into an art studio, and it was there that she worked her own brand of magic.

After bringing home books she'd found at the library's used book sale, Rosa turned what had been discarded into wreaths and keepsakes, into wedding centerpieces with hearts and flowers in profusion. She cut the centers from books and turned them into secret places to conceal mementos and treasures. Book pages were artfully folded to form sculpted words along the edges of the pages as though they had been carved. The creativity she demonstrated charmed and delighted me.

It was precise and painstaking work, hours and hours of it, and I soon found that it exacted a toll on her body that I had not anticipated. Between the stiff shoulders, aching wrists, and parched fingertips, this papercraft left its mark on her. I did what was possible within my constraints to assist, though she refused to use her final wish on this endeavor.

And with every passing day in her company, Rosa ensnared me more and more tightly in her web.

I wanted to blame the scent of roses, or the extraordinary color of her hair, or her lilting laugh when she teased me. She was naturally alluring to me in a way in which I was built to respond, and could not deny no matter how I tried. It was not artifice or manipulation that bound me to her beyond the invisible contract of the wishes.

It was Rosa herself.

In spite of the powers my position held, ascertaining the future was not one of them. Not for myself nor for anyone else. All I knew for certain was that Rosa captivated me more than anyone I had ever known.

"What would you like for breakfast this morning?" Rosa had asked the same question of me every morning for the past two weeks.

And my answer was likewise the same: "Whatever you would like."

It was true. I wanted what she wanted. I was never disappointed, and frequently pleased, by the results. Rosa had introduced me to the many delights of raspberry-stuffed French toast, waffles, and something called veggie hash that was surprisingly delicious. She truly enjoyed introducing me to new foods, watching me eat each bite with avid interest and a grin. The rest of the day was filled with the many tasks she had to do, but she insisted on starting the day with a leisurely and delicious meal.

I could not recall ever being cared for like this. Not coddled, for I was no child, but I could see how Rosa enjoyed cooking for me, encouraging me to savor the food she prepared, making note of those I especially loved.

I mattered to her. Not only for what I could do for her, but for who I was. And this was particularly perilous.

"You realize, of course, that you will be able to hire staff to deal with the business aspects of your venture," I said to her one afternoon as I watched her package and ready for delivery one of her finished pieces. Rosa did not care for this chore, or for the management of her website, or record keeping, but she persisted, nonetheless.

"I know. You keep reminding me." Was I getting on her nerves? Good. "Aside from having money coming in to pay anyone I hire—" She shot me a pointed look. "I need to know how all the moving parts work before I hand them off to someone else. And I need to let this play out longer so I can see if this is really going to work."

I *harrumphed* at her. Such doubts! "What will it take for you to believe that you will be successful?" I glowered, but it had no effect. My powers must be dimming in her prolonged company.

Rosa leaned back in her chair, the package resting on the postal scale. "I've had things go well before just to fall apart when I started to count on them. What if it happens with this?"

The thread of genuine concern in her voice was impossible to miss. She truly did not trust that this dream would remain once I departed, though I had had little to do with it thus far. What had happened to cause her to feel such distrust?

"Come with me." I held out my hand, though what possessed me to do so, I could not say. I led her down the stairs to her favorite seat in the living room, and moved to the kitchen to make her a cup of tea. She enjoyed the sweet mint brew while she relaxed at the end of the day, and I wanted her to relax enough to reveal what was holding her back. I went through the process of making the tea without the use of magic. I had long been cautioned against using magic in aid of a human outside of wish fulfillment, and I had always taken this advice seriously. While the act of doing small favors for Rosa did bind us more closely, I was long past caring. That ship, as they say, had long since sailed.

I placed the steaming cup into her hands, and settled into a chair across from her. She was pressed into the corner of the couch, her legs curled up on the cushion, and looking ever the picture of ease.

"What are your misgivings with regard to your venture?" I kept my voice light but reassuring, hoping she would confide in me, hoping I could allay those fears so that she could move forward.

And I could move on.

Rosa stared into the steaming mug for a long moment, as though searching the swirling liquid for answers. "I don't know."

Stuff and nonsense. "Do you doubt your talent?" I pressed. "Your sales prove your worth, do they not?"

Misgiving crept into her eyes. There was more here that my assurances could not dismiss.

"Do you not believe me?" I asked.

"No, I do." She blew a breath over the tea before taking a small sip. "The thing is, I always, *always* find a way to screw up."

Ah. Now we were making progress.

In my kindest, most reassuring tone, I demanded, "Tell me." And then, unbidden, I added, "Let me help."

Let me help? Other than words, there was nothing more I could *do* to help. Then she began to spin out her story.

"I'm sure you were at least a little curious about how I ended up on that mountain the night we met," she began.

True, unexpected though that curiosity was. I had never wondered such things about previous arrangements with my masters.

"I was so stupid," Rosa continued, her thumb tracing the curve of the mug's handle in a soothing rhythm. "I'd followed my boyfriend, Richie, here from Arizona. I thought I was in love." She scoffed at the notion, though I had no doubt that she had felt certain at the time. "I wasn't, not really. I was bored and restless with my life. And he'd promised that I'd have a good job waiting for me here, and we were going to have this grand adventure in Alaska. It was everything I'd dreamed of." Her sad, lopsided smile made my heart squeeze in sympathy. "I didn't mind starting over. It's not like I have family or anything great back home. But when I got here, the job had somehow 'been filled already.'" One-handed air quotes accompanied the phrase. "At least we had a place to live, even though it wasn't great, and cost more than I wanted to spend. I got a job at the same place where Richie worked, so I wasn't completely broke."

She looked up from her tea. "Did I mention I'd sold or given away a lot of my stuff before I left Arizona?"

I shook my head.

"Well, I did. I kept only what could fit in my car for the drive north. So, when I decided we were better off as friends and roommates, it wasn't a big deal because we still helped each other out. But then Richie stole from our employer. And not only did he get fired, but the spineless bastard also claimed I'd helped. I can really pick 'em, right?"

With this disclosure, I could not remain silent. "The fiend! He was further punished, I hope, and your honor restored."

"Not exactly." Her smile was slight, but her eyes warmed at my exclamation. "He now has a record for theft, and I wasn't arrested. But they refused to hire me back or give me a reference I could use to get another job." She paused to take a sip. "And it got worse, of course. He left Alaska—I don't know where he went, and I don't care—but I couldn't afford the apartment on my own or find a roommate in time before the landlord evicted me. That's how I ended up unemployed and living in my car."

"I am sorry. Richie did not deserve you. But why does that make you believe that you will not succeed now?"

"It's all about judgment. And apparently, I have lousy judgment. What if I hire someone who steals from me, or lies to me? What if I mess up my orders, or forget to pay my staff or my taxes? If I hire people, I'm responsible for them. What if I go out of business? Their lives will be affected too. If I make commitments, I have to see them through. What if I can't?"

The despair in her words broke my heart.

"Do you believe in your art?" I asked.

She did not hesitate. "Yes."

"Do you believe that you will do your absolute best?"

"Yes..." A little hesitation this time.

"Do you believe that I want you to succeed, and will do everything in my power to ensure that result?" I knew my powers were nullified in this instance, but I could—theoretically—do virtually anything a human might do to assist.

"Yes. I do." The certainty in her statement rocked me to my core.

"Then trust that I will not lead you astray, nor lie to you, nor mislead you. You *will* succeed, you *will* have the home you desire for as long as you like. I swear I will never let anything happen that might threaten your new life."

Was I wrong to use such strong language, promising things I would not be present to see through to the end? Perhaps. But it was only her lack of confidence that held her back at this point. If I could help to strengthen her belief in herself, I would do so unapologetically.

Rosa's face lit up, the glow everything I had hoped for. She placed her mug on the low table between us, and gestured for me to rise as she had. "Thank you, Ardeth." Would I ever tire of her calling me by the name she had bestowed? She moved forward to embrace me, her arms encircling my torso, pressing her cheek to my bare chest. "I'll never be able to thank you enough for all you've done for me."

Unbidden, my arms held her to me. I could feel the tickling sweep of her eyelashes as they brushed my skin when she blinked. "Your thanks are welcome, but completely unnecessary. I was only doing what I am meant to do."

Her answering smile plumped her cheek against me before she looked up to meet my eyes. Rosa was so beautiful in her joy. "No. I'm pretty sure you aren't compelled to listen to my most embarrassing mistakes and reassure me that things will get better."

She was not wrong, but I felt compelled to listen to her, to comfort her, to support her dreams. Not by virtue of our contract, but by the needs of my heart.

Rosa rose on her toes to place a kiss on my cheek, lingering beyond what might be considered chaste. It seemed we both were guilty of questionable judgment because I resisted no longer. I met her lips with mine, and changed everything.

9

ROSA

HE WAS KISSING ME. ARDETH WAS *KISSING* ME. AND I WAS kissing him back with everything I had pent up over the past two weeks.

My hands slid over his shoulders to tangle in the hair at his nape. God, I'd been wanting to do that since the night we'd met. I balanced on the tips of my toes to reach his mouth until he lifted me, urging me to wrap my legs around his waist. All the while, his mouth ate at mine as though I was the only food he could consume. We'd gone from a tame thank-you peck to ferocious tongue wrestling in the blink of an eye.

With unsurprising skill, Ardeth maneuvered around the coffee table to land gracefully on the couch without bumping into anything or dropping me, not that I would have noticed or let go of him. I was plastered to his chest, our lips exploring whatever skin either of us could reach. I got lucky on that score since he was already bare from the waist up. Or unlucky because I was wearing a big, fuzzy sweater.

Touches slowed, and our embrace became less frantic

but more intense, our energy channeled into one long, languid kiss. Instead of trying to crawl inside each other's skin, we melted into one another.

Somehow, I pulled back enough to focus my eyes. We were still breathing heavily, his chest rising and falling under me as I lay on top of him on the couch cushions. His lower lip, always full, was now plump and had a rosy tint to it, as if he had blood rushing close to the surface there. I wanted to take another nibble of that lip, but his eyes arrested me. He often wore this perpetually stern look, but now fire burned within. The warmth I'd seen sometimes when he looked at me was nothing compared to how his gaze incinerated me now.

"Rosa." Ardeth rasped my name as he shifted beneath me. I wanted to pin him down, continue my exploration—this time with our clothes off—but before I could put my mouth on him again, he'd already sat up and seated me next to him.

He pushed a hand through his mop of dark hair, mussed from my fingers. "Rosa," he began again, "I apologize for—"

"No," I practically shouted over him. "No. Don't you *dare* take this back. Don't you *dare* say you're sorry and wish this had never happened."

I wasn't going to let him push aside the attraction that had been simmering between us since the beginning. No way was he going to convince me that I didn't feel what I knew I felt. What I was certain we *both* felt.

With a grave nod, Ardeth took another tack. "This is not a wise course. You see that, surely."

"When is it ever?" I wanted so much to climb onto his lap, to curl up in his strong arms and stay there. He wasn't wrong.

"But this—us—it is the very definition of temporary."

"Temporary or not, we want each other. Badly." I took a chance, scooting closer to him. "You can't deny that." I gestured at his crotch.

He didn't even try to hide the erection tenting his loose pants. "It is not my intention to make your situation more difficult."

I huffed a laugh. "Trust me, taking care of my horniness is the opposite of making my situation difficult. You'd be doing me a favor."

Oops.

Ardeth's eyes took on a calculating glint, one I'd seen previously. "Is that your final wish? An evening of carnal pleasure with me? I can definitely make it worth the price."

Oh, hell no. I wasn't bargaining away a wish on sex, no matter how much I wanted him.

Some sixth sense told me he didn't want that either. Not if it meant he'd disappear immediately afterward. God, that would suck!

"Nuh uh," I said, waggling my finger in his face. "Nope. It's definitely *not* my final wish. But..." I trailed a hand down his magnificent chest. "That doesn't mean we can't take care of both our—" I glanced down at his still-significant erection. "Needs."

He caught my hand before it got farther than his abs, pressing it to his body. "You propose we slake our desires with each other with no expectation beyond momentary pleasure?"

Slake our desires? Fuck, yeah! "You can do that, right? Have sex with a human even if it isn't part of a wish?" Best to get all the details out in the open first. Ardeth had been an excellent tutor in that respect. "It's not forbidden or anything?"

The laugh that erupted from his throat rumbled

through my hand against his belly, and my fingers flexed under his. "No, it is not forbidden. I have pleasured and been pleasured by many in my time."

"Many, huh?" I had no interest in pursuing that line of questioning. "I assume you don't have any, you know, STIs. Or do djinn not get those? I mean, magic, so probably not. Must be nice. I don't have any, by the way. I got tested after I quit sleeping with Richie." I stopped, thinking further along those lines. "And pregnancy. Can you even have kids?" I could feel the blush push up my neck to my cheeks. My mouth was really running away from me.

"I can neither contract nor transmit any disease, nor can I impregnate humans." His fingertips lightly stroked the back of my hand in an almost meditative way, as though it helped him to focus on all the possibilities before us.

"Alrighty then." Leaning over, I kissed him, giving his lower lip a little suck as I pulled away. "Shall we?"

The wicked gleam in his hot, dark eyes lit the spark, but I burst into flames when he guided my hand to his straining hard-on. "Indeed, we shall."

10

ARDETH

I had told the truth when I had said that I had been sexually intimate with many. What I had not revealed was that all had been djinn, never human. Physical pleasure had been shared, but the relationships had not culminated in anything lasting. Consequently, I had committed to none.

Rosa seemed enthusiastic in her agreement to the temporary nature of this sensual union. I told myself that was reason enough to venture where I had not dared before.

I did not lie to her, but I was certainly lying to myself.

Lifting Rosa into my arms was as easy as breathing, her body soft and well cushioned where she pressed against my chest. Her lips, normally a pale pink, were darker and swollen from our kisses. I kissed her again and again, all while navigating our way up the stairs to the bedroom, so far lost in her that I bumped her feet into the wall as we entered her chambers.

A giggle escaped her at my clumsiness, and I swallowed that small bit of joy, wanting it all for myself. I wanted it all —-her happiness, her smiles, her sighs, and her moans.

I wanted every tiny piece of Rosa. And I would have it, at least for tonight.

Striding to the bed, I gently laid her down. There was no need to rush, and I had every desire to savor, and to encourage Rosa to do likewise. I wondered if her past lovers had been attentive to her needs, if she had been pleasured as she deserved. Whether they had or not, I vowed to make our time together memorable.

But Rosa was impatient, pulling at my shoulders, urging me down to her. I allowed her to take my mouth, her silken tongue stroking against mine. Ending the kiss, I reached out and combed her astonishing hair with my fingers. It shone the darkest red in the soft light of the bedside lamp, spread out atop the pillow like a river of rubies.

"You have a thing for my hair," she murmured, a half smile on her lips.

"Mmm, I do." I raked my fingers through her locks once more, the cool length of it belying its fiery appearance.

"Well," she said, sitting up and ruining my efforts to turn her hair into a crimson fan, "I have a thing for you and that fine body of yours." With that proclamation, she flung her sweater over her head and across the room. "You can play with my hair later."

"Promise?" But my gaze was captured by her bounteous breasts, full and enticingly framed by her undergarment. I cupped them in my hands, tracing the fabric's edge with a finger. Her skin was so soft, smoother than rose petals. I followed my finger with my tongue, desiring to learn if she tasted of roses as well.

She did not, but that was by no means a disappointment.

I needed to see for myself the color of her nipples. Were they the same pale pink of her unkissed lips? Or were they darker?

Fumbling at her back, I could not discern how to release her from the garment. With a laugh, Rosa took pity on me, or perhaps it was something more like impatience, and freed her breasts from their confinement.

Oh, they were everything I had hoped, their tips bunched tight like tiny rosebuds, several shades deeper than her lips. Lowering her to the mattress, I made a leisurely exploration of her breasts, licking, sucking, nuzzling them. Her breath came with sighs, her small hands pinned my head to her as I worried a peak with my teeth.

"Does this please you?" I glanced up to see her hazel eyes, the color of old gold in this light, and she blinked before she answered.

"Yes," she gasped. I nipped the lower curve of her breast. "More."

If Rosa wanted more, more I would give.

As she pulled me by my hair up to meet her mouth, our kisses sloppy with need, I climbed completely onto the bed, settling between her legs. I dwarfed her. I propped myself on my forearms so as not to crush her with my weight, but she clung to me, wrapping her legs around me and grinding her hips into mine.

I was used to denying myself pleasure for long periods, and I intended to wait until Rosa had reached her climax several times before taking my own, but her sounds, her grasping hands, the way her legs shifted restlessly against me made it impossible to ignore my throbbing cock. Keeping my trousers on was an almost futile effort to rein in my impulses.

My mouth traced a path down the center of her body, through the valley between her heavy breasts, across her soft belly with its tender indent of a navel. I dipped my tongue into that tiny well, and felt her stomach quiver.

"More," she moaned, and it was all I wanted as well. More. More of this, more of her.

More freedom. More time.

Her hands pushed at the crown of my head. I could take a hint as well as any man.

Better.

My large fingers unbuttoned her trousers with difficulty, but the rest were dispatched with ease, both of us eager to have her body completely bare. The last of her garments were flung over the side of the bed, and I could finally feast on the sight I had dreamt of for endless nights.

Her skin glowed in the lamplight, a sharp contrast to the emerald velvet of the bed coverings. I swallowed hard, trying to slow my breaths as I reveled in the knowledge that she was mine. For tonight, Rosa was mine.

Slowly, so slowly, I traced my hands from her dainty toes, along her arches to slender ankles, up well-formed calves to a hitherto unknown ticklish spot behind her knees. Her rounded thighs led to plush hips between which lay a tuft of dark-red curls.

"Now you." Rosa leaned up on her elbows, her tongue tracing her lower lip. "I want to see all of you."

If I removed my trousers now, the thread of my control would surely break. "Not yet. I have more of you still to see."

Scooping my hands under her ample buttocks, I gave them a squeeze as I pulled her to the edge of the mattress and propped her feet on the edge. It was not necessary to nudge her knees apart; Rosa spread them willingly, eagerly, wanting this as much as I.

The perfume from her center wafted up, rich and heady. There should exist a flower that smelled like her, one that could be cultivated and distilled into a perfume so that I could enjoy it the rest of my days. It made my head spin in the best way. Rosa was Temptation personified; I would not rest until I had tasted her and committed her to memory.

Placing kisses from her knee to the crease of her thigh, I could feel her muscles tensing with anticipation of my mouth on her nether lips as I placed her leg over my shoulder. I moved to the other knee, mirroring my actions and prolonging our mutual torture. The closer I got to her center, the less resistance I had to offer. I buried my nose in her ruby curls, inhaling deeply and smiling while she shoved at my head.

My lusty woman.

At long last, I reached out my tongue to finally taste of her essence, drinking from her well of delight. I was truly lost, unable to restrain myself any longer. I lapped at her as though dying of thirst in the desert, plunging my tongue into her, then teasing her plump bud with flicks. Her swollen folds were the same rosy hue as her nipples, beautiful and perfect. Rosa's hips lifted in tandem with the rhythmic stroke of my tongue, and her whimpers became moans as she neared her climax.

My hands were so large compared to her channel, but she welcomed my thick finger, then a second, into her soft heat as I continued to lash at her swollen nub. Crooking my fingers, I stroked her and felt her inner muscles spasm around me. She was close, and I would deliver to her that sweet release. I closed my lips around her bud, sucked, and her whine dissolved into a wordless cry as she came on my hand and mouth.

Softly, I brought her pleasure through to the end, the very last tremor in her body dissipating as she sank, limp, onto the mattress. I sucked her nectar from my fingers, relishing the taste I would always associate with her. The only sounds were our gusting breaths, and the pounding of the blood in my ears as I held off my own climax.

One day, this image of Rosa—flushed and replete, wantonly splayed atop a background of emerald velvet, fiery hair tumbled across a snow-white pillow—would keep me warmer than any flame ever could.

11

ROSA

HOLY SHIT. THAT WAS...MAGICAL.

I was pretty sure Ardeth didn't actually use magic on me, but his tongue was pure enchantment, and not in a Disney sort of way.

More like a PornHub sort of way.

I was still recovering from my orgasm, but I couldn't wait another second to finally see all of him. I'd waited too long already, relying only on my imagination when I got myself off before falling asleep every night. I wanted to see him with my own eyes, touch him with my own hands, and make him come as hard as he'd just made me.

I managed to clumsily scoot my ass back up the bed so it wasn't hanging off, and sat up to see Ardeth running his tongue along his lips, licking up my juices with a drunk look on his face.

I've never felt so desirable, so completely sexy after being eaten out in my entire life. He did that to me with the greedy smack of his lips.

"Come here," I said, patting the bed next to me. "Let me taste."

You'd have thought I'd just lit a bonfire behind his eyes, he looked at me with such heat. He all but launched himself at me, eating at my mouth the same way he'd eaten my pussy. I could taste myself on his tongue, on his chin where he hadn't cleaned it off. Underneath was the flavor of Ardeth.

Two great tastes that taste great together, that was me and Ardeth. And I couldn't get enough.

But I had to put my hands on him, my mouth too. I needed to see his big, gorgeous body without anything covering him. And I desperately needed him inside me. Like, yesterday. But I also wanted to make him feel cherished.

I had a full night's work ahead of me. And I'd never been so eager to clock in for duty.

"Off." I pushed at his shoulders until I saw a wariness in his eyes. "Not you. Take *them* off." I gestured at the loose trousers that were now pitching a full-on circus tent. Would I be able to handle all of him if he was built to scale? I mean, he was close to seven feet tall. What if his dick was eighteen inches and as thick as a baseball bat?

Never mind. I'd figure something out. At least we wouldn't need to find a condom to fit.

Ardeth stood, and took one drawstring in his hand. "Would you like to do it?"

"I would be honored." I scooted to the edge of the bed, sitting with my knees under me. He handed me the drawstring like it was unwrapped around a package, which I suppose was true. *Merry early Christmas to me!* I pulled as slowly as I could make myself do, my eyes never straying from his crotch, but completely aware of Ardeth's hawklike gaze on my face.

I hoped I didn't disappoint, because he sure as hell didn't. Not that he ever could, not by any measure.

The drawstring loosened, his trousers dropped to the floor, and he kicked them aside. His cock was...well, it was enormous, naturally. And blue, like the rest of him, but with that telltale ruddiness underneath. If I hadn't wanted him so badly, I suppose I could have had cautionary thoughts. As it was, my eyes must have bugged out because Ardeth immediately attempted to soothe my supposed fears.

"I know it is larger than an average human male organ," he began in a rush.

Releasing a nervous laugh, I tried reassuring him. "No, it's fine, really. It's just...ginormous." What else could I say? There was no denying what was right here in front of us. "We can do this." To myself, I muttered, "*I* can do this."

"Wait, Rosa. There is one bit of magic I can use without running afoul of the restrictions." Ardeth closed his eyes, and slowly passed his hands, fingers extended, in front of his groin. When his hands moved back to his sides, his cock had downsized considerably, but was still too large for me to handle without discomfort.

"Um, just a smidge smaller, please." I hated to look a gift horse in the dick, but since he was willing to accommodate, we might as well go all the way, right?

One quick adjustment later, and Ardeth was absolutely perfect—big, but not so much that we'd have to worry about injuries instead of pleasure.

"I'd like to program this setting for future use," I said, nodding approvingly.

He answered as expected and with a grin. "Is that your final wish?"

"Nope." I crooked my finger, beckoning him to me. "Come here. It's my turn."

When he got within reach, I put my hands on his hips—*holy shit, this man's ass was a masterpiece*—and pulled him closer. His cock bobbed before I captured it in my hand, my fingers encircling him.

Ardeth had to have rock-solid self-esteem to voluntarily choose shrinkage. And while that doesn't sound sexy on its own, the fact that he'd done it for me, for my comfort and pleasure, and ignored any blow to his ego? That was insanely sexy, and more than a little endearing.

He had a raw sexuality combined with disarming charm that I found irresistible.

In return for his sacrifice, I was going to do my best to give him at least a fraction of the pleasure he had just given me.

I wrapped my lips around the head of his cock, relaxed my tongue, and took as much of him into my mouth as I could. The groan from deep inside him even resonated through his cock, assuring me how much he loved it. I pulled him out, and licked him like a lollipop. Now, *this* I could do all day. I dragged my tongue along his length, watching him watch me, and felt my pussy getting wetter. God, I was a goner for his hot eyes on me. If I were wearing panties, they would have incinerated.

More than anything, I wanted Ardeth to feel wanted, appreciated, desired for more than what he could give. A treasure like this man—this djinn—should know his innate worth was recognized. And I was going to do my damndest to get that message across.

My hands were trying to make up for the deficit of my small mouth, but it didn't seem to make any difference to Ardeth. I palmed his balls as I tongued at his slit, the flavor of him different from anything I'd ever tasted. He started to thrust through my hands, and I worked to keep up. He was obviously trying hard to hold back, hips bucking when he couldn't hold still any longer.

I could say the same as I squirmed, my thighs pressed against his knees at the edge of the mattress.

"Enough," he commanded, his voice booming through the room. "I need you. Now."

Apparently, that commanding voice really did it for me. He could demand almost anything of me, and I'd snap to.

I moved over so he could join me on the bed. "I think I should be on top."

I hadn't seen that imperious eyebrow lately, but it put in a surprise appearance. I hadn't realized how much it turned me on until I felt a trickle of moisture on my thighs.

"Do you?" he drawled.

Rather than answer, I pushed him onto his back. If I were being honest, I'd admit he allowed me to push him down. "You're still so big, I want to adjust at my own speed," I explained.

He nodded, giving in willingly, and placed his hands behind his head. While his posture was relaxed, Ardeth's eyes were locked on me with an intensity that stole my breath. If he hadn't already stolen my heart, that moment would have sealed the deal.

On my knees, I straddled his hips. I dragged his cock along my slit, getting it wet before notching it at my entrance. Slowly, so slowly, I sank down onto him, taking the head inside before pausing to acclimate to his thickness.

Ardeth's biceps flexed, and his jaw clenched, making his features appear sharper. His nostrils flared as I sank down yet another inch, but he kept his body still. Inch by deliciously excruciating inch, I lowered myself onto him. The tension he held inside was obvious when I leaned my hands on his pecs. They were like quivering stone.

Between Ardeth's magical adjustments and my prompts, we'd managed to get it right. I was fuller than I'd ever been, but it was Ardeth—this beautiful, giving man—who set my heart racing.

I closed my eyes, pushing back on the flood of emotion that welled within me. It wouldn't do to start sobbing just as we reached the good part. He might stop, and then I'd cry for other reasons.

Opening my eyes, I lost myself in the depth of his gaze, the crinkle of concentration between his brows, the tension in his jaw.

I rose up, then rocked back down, ending the down-stroke with a dirty grind of my hips that brought a moan from my mouth. Ardeth's hands went to my hips, stilling me.

"What?" I asked.

"I do not...." He took a deep breath. "I want to last."

I nodded.

"And I want to fuck you now."

I nodded more vigorously this time.

Ardeth unleashed himself and became a whirlwind of sensation. His hands on my hips, his cock in my pussy, the sounds he made, words I couldn't even understand. He took over, raising me to where only the tip of his cock was still in, and then plunging me back down, ending with a grind of his pelvis against my clit. All I could do was hang on, like being on a roller coaster, the anticipation of climbing to the top, then the rush of hitting the bottom, but this ride had all the fireworks too.

As the pace sped up, I held on to his arms and trusted he would get us there. Each pump, every time my clit slid against his skin, I climbed closer to my release. What would happen when I came around him? No sooner had the thought raced through my mind when my orgasm fired through me like a comet. I wasn't a screamer, but my lungs let loose a sound I barely recognized as my own. The rhythm became erratic as he reached his own climax, slamming me down on him as he pumped his own hips up to meet me. He bellowed as he came, his fingers dimpling my hips. I was a rag doll in his arms, draped over him as the last shudders passed through his magnificent body.

So worth it. No matter what happened, I would never regret this night, nor the man who held me as though I was cherished.

And I knew I would never be the same again.

12

ROSA

It hadn't escaped my notice that Ardeth and I had been playing a strange game of chicken since my second wish was enacted. He hinted and cajoled and maneuvered to try to get me to spell out my last wish. And I dodged his traps, diverted his attention, and straight up avoided answering him.

As we'd grown more intimate with each other, Ardeth had stopped pushing, both of us reluctant to address the magical elephant in the room. I wanted to believe it had something to do with the sex we'd been having, and the closeness developing between us.

I didn't want him to disappear from my life. But I couldn't ignore the possibility that I might be holding him here against his will.

One afternoon, we were in the library, sitting together on the couch in front of the fire, watching the chickadees at the bird feeder outside the window. Our teacups sat on the low table, steaming and fragrant.

"Ardeth," I began, watching as his strong fingers

massaged my forearm, sore from folding and cutting book pages, "why me?"

"Why you?" He peered up at me through his dark lashes.

"Why did you choose to grant my wishes instead of someone else's? I mean, there are plenty of people who deserve it more than me."

His grip moved to my hand, gentling as he worked my palm. "There is neither rhyme nor reason to it that I have ever seen. I have served those who are selfish and unkind, even cruel. I do not know how I have been brought into their paths any more than I know why I was brought into yours. Why do you ask?"

"It just seems like there should be some sort of system, you know? That the chance for good fortune should come only to people who deserve it."

"You have expressed similar sentiments previously. I thought we had laid them to rest." Taking my other hand, Ardeth looked into my eyes, all earnest and understanding. "Fate ordains, and questioning changes nothing. The why of it does not matter so much as what you choose to do with the opportunity. That much I can say for certain."

"You believe in fate, then?" I asked. I'd never been one to subscribe to that kind of thinking, but Ardeth had seen and experienced things I never would. Maybe it wasn't just a superstitious idea.

"I do."

"Then why would it be your destiny to cater to people like me? Don't you hate having to serve people for centuries, always doing what *they* want instead of following your own path?"

Frankly, it sounded like a miserable existence to me.

Setting my hand gently in my lap, Ardeth sat back

against the sofa, his eyes sharp and unfathomable. Minutes passed, thick and slow, before he finally spoke.

"This has always been my path. I have known no other. Why is it my destiny? Again, questioning changes nothing. I accept it for what it is."

His dismissal only made me more persistent. "But don't you ever wish you could do what *you* want? Have control over your time, your actions, your future?"

Maybe I was looking for absolution from him, confirmation that my delays didn't cause him pain or resentment. Or some declaration from Ardeth that he wished to remain with me as well. Was I any better than anyone else if I kept him here against his will?

"Rosa." Ardeth took my hand once more, his voice gentle. "I have not always liked where I have been, or what I have been required to do, but can you not say the same? Would you change your life so that you never experienced any unfortunate situations?"

I pondered his words as he worked on my other forearm and hand, caring for me as no one had before. I was truly fortunate, even spoiled. Since Ardeth had entered my life, I had not only everything I needed, but also everything I wanted. The only thing that would make it better would be knowing Ardeth and I had a shot at forever.

It was time to come clean with him, even if it meant hearing bad news. "Maybe not. But I know you need me to make my last wish so you can move on because it's your job. And I shouldn't keep you here if you want to go."

Ardeth placed a tender kiss on my palm. "I am content to stay for as long as you need. I am where I want to be."

"Thank you." I leaned over to kiss him, so grateful to have him with me.

"I owe you thanks, as well," he replied, tucking a stray

lock of hair behind my ear before leaning close. "You have excited such emotion in me. My heart is full in ways it never has been before." Kissing my palm, he pressed it to his chest. "I want you to continue calling me Ardeth, but I am ready...I *want* to tell you my name, the one by which I am known amongst my kind."

His breath was warm on my ear as he whispered a name I would never repeat.

"Wow." If I'd known so much was riding on it, maybe I would have given it a little more thought first, and not named him after a movie character just because of a resemblance to the actor. "I'm honored that you trust me enough to share it with me."

"I do. I trust you implicitly." With a smile, he reached for his cup of tea.

His hand passed right through it.

At first, I wasn't sure what I'd seen. I'd been staring at patterns in folded pages for hours already that day, and maybe my eyes were strained. But Ardeth froze, as shocked as I was.

"Did...." I paused until Ardeth met my eyes. "Did your hand just go through your cup?"

Neither of us moved, as though unnecessary motion might cause something worse to happen.

"Yes." I'd never seen his eyes so wide, the whites showing stark around his dark irises. "It did."

"Why? Why did it do that?" What I really wanted to know was how to make sure it didn't happen again, but I was afraid of the answer.

I was right to be afraid.

"It is unusual, unprecedented really, for me to take so long to grant all three wishes. My stay here is causing my power to wane."

Shit.

"This is my fault, isn't it? I caused this because I'm taking too long to make my last wish." I grabbed his hand, anxious to know it was solid, relieved to feel his grip on my fingers firm and strong.

He shook his head. "You are not to blame, Rosa."

"Ardeth, tell me the truth." I swiveled, drawing my legs under me, and grasping both his hands in mine. "If I had made my wish a week ago, would you be weakening now?"

The sorrow in his eyes brought tears to mine. "No."

"Then I need to make my wish," I declared.

"No!" Ardeth scooped me onto his lap, wrapping his arms around me. "Not yet. I'm not ready to leave."

"I'm not ready for you to go, either." I pressed my cheek to his warm chest, my tears making him damp. "But you can't go unless you can grant my wish, and you'll keep growing weaker. Is there a chance you'll become too weak to save yourself?"

He rubbed his cheek against my hair before answering. "It is possible. Perhaps even likely. I do not know for certain. I heard a story once, long, long ago, of a djinn whose master wanted to ensure that no one would ever receive a wish from that djinn ever again. He refused to state his final wish, and the djinn eventually faded away into nothingness. I believed it was only a tale meant to spur my kind to conclude our business with speed. I never believed it could be true."

Ardeth pulled away and kissed my nose. I gave a watery hiccup, and the gentleness in his eyes only made me sob harder.

"Shhh, my sweet, do not cry." Holding me close, Ardeth did his best to soothe me, but I wasn't having it.

"I want you to stay, but I can't stand the thought of you

just...vanishing. I won't let that happen to you, Ardeth. I won't." Grasping his beautifully stern face in my hands, I kissed him. "I love you. I won't let you die."

He kissed me back, all tenderness and grief and longing for a future we couldn't have. "It will not happen today, nor tomorrow, but soon. I want nothing more than to spend as much time as I have left with you before I grant your final wish."

"How will you know when you've reached the limit of your power being drained? How can you be sure we won't wait too long?" I needed reassurance, something solid to hold on to. If I couldn't get a definitive answer from him, I would be forced to give him my wish now.

Tonight.

"I will know. Now that I understand what I was sensing, I can monitor how quickly my power wanes."

"Promise me you won't wait too long." I may have gripped his cheeks a bit roughly. "Promise me."

"I promise." One more kiss before he swept me up into his arms as he stood. "We will not waste one moment we have left."

Then he carried me upstairs to our bedroom.

13

ARDETH

The light of the fire flickered over Rosa's curtain of hair, glinting a bloodred against the snowy white of the pillow as she drowsed in my arms. Smoothing an errant tendril behind her ear, I traced the sweet curve of her cheek, unable to recall with any clarity a time when I had felt so at peace. Surely such a time must exist, but I could not call it forth from my past.

My memory was long, my life even longer, yet I was certain that this night—this woman—would remain within easy recall for the rest of my days. I could only hope that Rosa's heart would mend after my departure. My own was in peril. While I had many regrets, she would never be one of them.

There was one comfort I took from our predicament. Being human, Rosa's life was substantially shorter than my own, a mere blink in time. She would not mourn the loss of our bond as long as I. I would miss her to the depths of my soul for all my days to come. Even so, I would not trade one moment with her. The joy of loving Rosa would forever be worth the pain of losing her.

Rosa squirmed, nuzzling her face against my shoulder before settling peacefully once more. I needed sleep to conserve my energy, but I intended to spend this night memorizing each detail of her, cementing it in my mind.

I twisted a lock of her hair around my finger, then let it loose to drape across her pale cheek, along her slender neck. The color of her hair was unusual, neither black nor red, but a unique shade even I had never seen before. It was exactly the color of the midnight-red roses in the gardens of the old woman in Bucharest—

My breath caught in my throat as I stared in shock at the glorious woman in my arms.

Roses. Rosa.

The memory flooded in, swamping me in disbelief.

It had been perhaps six hundred years earlier when I had found myself with a soothsayer for a mistress. She had summoned me deliberately, but she had been neither cruel nor greedy in her requests, selecting wishes to make the lives of the people of her village better rather than for personal gain.

She had wasted neither my time nor her own, making her wishes with alacrity over the course of a summer night in her garden. Deep-red roses the color of blood climbed along the back garden wall, their fragrance heady in the sultry air as she sat on a cold stone bench. Before she would reveal her last wish, releasing me from my bond, she bestowed upon me—or cursed me with—a prophecy concerning my own fate. I scoffed, disbelieving that she had any such skill or talent as might pertain to my kind. I knew my future as well as I knew my past: it was to serve those who summoned until they completed their triad of requests, and then move to the next, on and on until the end of my very long existence.

The soothsayer declared that I would tread a different path. One with passion, and unbearable bliss. I would fall helplessly in love with a woman with hair like those roses in the garden.

Rosa.

That I would make a choice that was not a choice at all.

And then, my life would come to an end.

I believed in fate. I had seen prophecies and predictions come true many times. Fate was absolute; I knew this to be fact. It could not be dodged, nor hidden from, nor ignored when it came knocking. Despite my many years, I had never been in love. I had long believed I never would be, that it was my particular fate to always be alone. While djinn do eventually die, it is more as the shadow of night is replaced by the dawn, a gradual diminishing rather than an abruptly-snuffed candle. A human life was the span of a breath to djinn, and my world was not one a human could inhabit.

This was truly an impossible situation.

I was djinn, and I was in love.

With the woman with hair like midnight roses.

With Rosa, my sweet, exquisite Rosa, asleep in my arms, oblivious to her place in the tapestry of fate.

14

ROSA

After an amazing night with Ardeth, I expected to wake up and continue from where we'd left off, pausing for breakfast and then climbing back in bed again. All I wanted was to be with him, touching him, kissing him, feeling his skin against mine, his low voice rumbling in my ear.

I was in love. Absolutely, ass over teakettle in love.

Too bad it took something as drastic as Ardeth's inability to grasp a teacup to make me say the words.

I think I'd known for a while, but what was the point if he was going to leave once I made my last wish? Talk about an expiration date. I don't know if it was cowardice, or cleverness, or just plain stubbornness, but I had refused to make that wish until I absolutely had to. Knowing now what it was costing Ardeth to stay, though...I wouldn't be able to hold off much longer.

My wish was for Ardeth to stay with me. Was that even possible? I felt like breathing that aloud would be asking for trouble. I didn't even know if he would want that too. He'd said he wanted to spend as much time with me as possible before leaving, but I couldn't assume that meant the rest of our lives, or at least mine.

In an effort to distract myself, I threw myself into my work, my art. My awareness of his presence in the room never left me, no matter how immersed I was, but I couldn't think of anything else to do. I worked until I couldn't, then Ardeth fed me, and we crawled into bed, losing ourselves in each other, making love until I couldn't keep my eyes open any longer.

After three days of crafting, I was ready to drop and my fingers were sore and laced with papercuts. Ardeth pressed me to take a break, convincing me to go out for a walk for some fresh air and exercise. Though he didn't need to, we bundled up against the cold, Ardeth in a wool peacoat and me in a down jacket. Using his magic to cloak himself in invisibility would deplete his remaining strength, but a tall, blue, half-naked man might freak out the neighbors if we ran into someone walking their dog. We made our way toward the pond at the end of the street.

The air was crisp, the sky blue, and the sun made the hoarfrost on the trees sparkle. This was my first winter somewhere cold, and it was as magical as I'd imagined.

"You are not thinking about work, are you?"

"Not even a little," I assured him.

"Good." He squeezed my hand with his. "There is no need to toil so relentlessly. While success will not be immediate, it *will* come, I promise you."

"Yeah, yeah, a marathon, not a sprint. I know." My eye roll earned a scowl, which made me smile in return.

Our feet crunched across the snow, the sound louder in the cold as we passed through the wooded area between the street's dead end and the pond. The flat, frozen surface gleamed, perfect for skating, if only I had ice skates and knew how to use them. Growing up in Arizona hadn't provided me with those skills. We stopped at the edge, looking across the expanse of ice.

I threw myself at Ardeth, wrapping my arms around his chest. Tipping my head back and squinting into the bright sunlight, I invited his kiss. He responded, the warmth of his lips in sharp contrast to the chill of the air, our breath combining in great clouds around our heads.

His kiss was all tenderness and caring, as though we had all the time in the world. But I knew better. It hadn't escaped my notice that his powers were changing, that he was growing weaker with each passing day. He didn't want to talk about it. The longer we put off the last wish, the weaker he would become. I would have to make a choice soon, but I needed to find some way to use the wish to keep Ardeth with me, or at least give him that option.

We had both needed this little break, this time out in the larger world. Whatever happened, I knew I would love Ardeth forever. For now, today, at this moment, that was enough.

The brilliant sun made the snow look like it had diamonds embedded, glinting so that it was almost blinding. There was nowhere else I wanted to be but here. A sudden giddiness overtook me, equal parts joy and adoration for the man—djinn—holding me. I drew away from his embrace, smiling up at him. "Have you ever gone sliding across the ice?"

His mouth curved up, but he shook his head. "No, I cannot say that I have. Have you?"

"No, never." I turned and ran for the smooth patch of ice, glancing over my shoulder. "Well, what are you waiting for? Come on!"

My boots found less traction once I left the shore, but I

gained momentum until I made myself slide sideways, squealing, about six feet. Not great, but not bad considering I was wearing boots with tread and not more slippery footwear.

"Rosa, be careful!" Ardeth called out, taking only a few steps forward. "It may not be safe."

"It's fine." I slid again, this time only four feet since I had less momentum on the ice. "Try it!"

I did a less than graceful twirl, hoping to entice him to join me, only to hear the crack of the ice and Ardeth's shout of alarm a second before I plunged into the frigid water.

15

ARDETH

My heart stopped when I heard the resounding snap of the ice breaking apart under Rosa's feet. With a shout, I flung out my magic with every bit of strength I could muster, only to feel it falter short of catching her. The tethered force fizzled, useless and wasted.

I raced out onto the ice, not caring if the surface would bear my weight as long as I reached Rosa. I would give anything, everything, to have her safe again. The ice made faint cracklings as I got closer to the hole that had swallowed her, so I lowered myself to my belly and crawled to the edge where ice met water.

Rosa had not yet surfaced for air. I shouted her name incessantly, searching for any sign of her. If she was trapped beneath the ice, unable to breathe or to reach out a hand, how would I pull her out?

Not knowing if it would help but desperate to try anything at all, I plunged my arm into the water, carefully moving it as I searched for her by touch. My hand quickly became numb with cold and I panicked, imagining how Rosa must feel, caught in the icy hold of the pond. Her name became interspersed with prayers and pleas to spare her, to take me instead, to let her live.

My voice reduced to a hoarse whisper, I closed my eyes to focus all my concentration on my frozen fingertips. Finally, after an eternity of panic and despair, my hand brushed something in the water, and I grasped greedily at it, pulling upward toward the surface. My fist emerged, wrapped around bloodred hair, and Rosa's too pale face followed.

Her eyes were closed, her skin waxy, as I wedged my hands under her arms and levered her onto the ice. There was no breath creating clouds above her still lips, as blue as my own. On instinct more than knowledge, I pressed firmly low on her chest, feebly hoping to somehow push the water out of her lungs, to force her to breathe and talk and live.

Whether by my efforts or some other force, with a watery gurgle, Rosa sputtered and coughed up the fluid inside. Rolling her to her side and cradling her head, I sent up words of thanks and promises of I knew not what.

But the danger had not passed. She was soaked through, her skin frigid. I needed to get her warm again, or I could still lose her.

Not wanting to risk both of us falling through the ice, and not trusting the surface to hold me with Rosa in my arms, I carefully dragged her prone body to the shore before picking her up. Once I had her safely on dry land, I ran, trying not to trip on the tussocks of grass hidden under the snow that surrounded the pond. Every bit of strength I had left carried us home.

After assuring myself that she still breathed—her eyes were closed, and she did not speak—I placed Rosa on the floor in front of the fireplace in the library. I undressed her, tossing her sodden garments aside. I removed my own soggy coat as well. I paused only to light the fire and to retrieve a towel from the bathroom so I could chafe her cold skin and dry her wet hair.

When I had done all I could think to do, and yet still she was chilled to the bone, I moved her to the couch in front of the fire, and tucked a blanket around her body.

Then I collapsed onto the floor, and knew nothing more.

16

ROSA

I was cold, so cold. Naked under a blanket. When I opened my eyes, I discovered I was on the couch in the library. I could hear the fire crackling in the fireplace, and the mantel clock ticking as always. My lungs felt tight, and I erupted into a coughing fit when I tried to take a deep breath.

How did I get here? The last thing I remembered, I was out on the pond, tempting Ardeth to join me on the ice. Then it cracked and I—

Ardeth must have pulled me out, saving my life. Of course, he had.

I struggled to sit up, rubbing at my irritated eyes. "Ardeth?" Swinging my legs off the couch to stand, my feet bumped something on the floor. "Ardeth!"

He lay collapsed next to the couch, pale as the surface of a glacier, only the barest tint of blue to his skin. I fell to my knees beside him, fumbling to find his pulse. I knew what his heartbeat sounded like, so surely he would have a pulse if he were alive.

He had to be alive.

Finding no pulse, and feeling no breath coming from his mouth and nose, I started chest compressions as I'd been taught back when I had spent a summer lifeguarding at the YMCA pool. I lost track of time, arm muscles burning as I chanted, "Come back, come back to me." I didn't know how long I kept it up before my arms gave out completely, but I pleaded with God, Allah, whatever celestial being might listen: "Please give me my last wish. Give me Ardeth."

Then I sagged against him, dry sobs racking my ruined lungs.

I had lost him. I had finally found the love of my life, and he was gone.

Pulling his too-still body to me, I rocked Ardeth as though he were a sleeping child instead of my dead lover. His body still radiated warmth, even after what must have been—

Wait. That seemed...odd. Wrong. Was Ardeth warmer now than when I had started CPR? I couldn't tell. I had been so cold when I'd started chest compressions, and I'd worked up a frantic sweat doing them. But he was certainly warmer than a dead human would be.

Did djinn turn warm rather than cold when they died? Somehow, I'd imagined that they would disappear into thin air, with no body left behind to show they had ever existed.

My hands stroked over his chest, his arms, his beloved face. He was freaking *warm*. And his skin, such an icy blue before, was slowly taking on a golden hue, as if he had suddenly spent time on a sunny beach.

I had no idea what to think. This was bizarre, and heartbreaking, and Ardeth didn't even look like himself anymore since he'd started...goldening.

I checked his pulse again, but it remained still. With his

heart not beating, his breath not gusting from his lips, did any of the other changes matter? Not to me.

Grabbing the blanket, I covered both of us, snuggling up to Ardeth's ever-warming body. A different cold took me over, this time from the inside.

It was so unfair. Ardeth had saved me—not once, but twice—and I couldn't do the same for him. I had my forever home, I had the beginnings of a career I wanted, but I no longer had the one thing I would have traded all of that for. Ardeth. Love. A life with the very best man I would ever know.

And I'd lost the chance to make a life with Ardeth my last wish.

It would remain a mystery whether he would have been able or allowed to grant it, but even if he couldn't, at least he would have known how important he was to me.

"I love you, Ardeth," I whispered. "I will always love you." I kissed his forehead, his cheeks and—one last time—his lips. "Goodbye."

17

ARDETH

I woke to the sensation of Rosa's soft lips on mine and the sound of her tearful voice saying, "Goodbye."

She could not leave me. Not now.

"Stay," I croaked. My lips moved before my eyelids fluttered open to see Rosa, mouth agape with shock.

It is not every day one comes back from the dead.

"You're alive? *You're alive!*" She could not have held me tighter if she had been a serpent. "I don't know how, but—" Rosa interrupted herself to kiss me again, one cool hand stroking my hair back from my face. "You know you were dead, right?"

My Rosa, always removing any ambiguity.

"I believe so," I replied, nodding. I struggled to sit up against the couch, and caught sight of my hand, my arm, my chest. My skin had changed; I appeared as though I were a lightly tanned human, no longer my customary shade of azure.

"Yeah, pretty freaky, right?" Rosa traced a hand from my shoulder to my wrist before lacing her fingers with mine. "You got really warm even though your heart wasn't beating, and your skin changed color. Almost like the opposite of humans when they die. Weird." She raised our joined hands to her lips, placing a kiss on my palm. "But I'll take it."

"And you? Are you well?" I asked, worried about the lasting effects of her near drowning. "I did not have an opportunity to be certain before I...expired."

"You saved me, Ardeth. You gave your life for mine." Rosa's bottom lip trembled as she tried to smile. "Did you use your magic to pull me out of the water? I don't remember anything after I fell in."

"No, beloved." Would the outcome have been different if my powers had not abandoned me in that moment? I would never know. "I had no magic left to use in your aid."

"You pulled me out yourself, and brought me back here. Probably used up all your strength, didn't you." It was not a question at all. She already knew the answer.

"So it would seem."

The blanket had slipped to her waist, baring her beautiful breasts to my thirsting eyes. It was too soon after our mutual demise for such a distraction.

"Rosa, if you are strong enough and warmed through, perhaps we could put on clean, dry clothing before I tell you a story you need to hear."

We got dressed, and made a pot of tea to sip while I related the prophecy I had kept from her. I had never dreamed, if dream I could, that the soothsayer's prediction would come to pass in such a startling and beneficent way.

"Holy wow!" Rosa was nestled in my arms before the fire in the library, our tea forgotten as my tale came to an end. "The old woman said you'd fall in love and die, but didn't tell you that you'd come alive again? What a cliffhanger!"

I chuckled at her theatrical tone. "Just because a prophet can see the future does not necessarily mean that they see every detail. Some events are not meant to be fully known before they come to pass. For example, I certainly did not anticipate falling in love with you."

Rosa beamed, her smile a gift I would always treasure. "You love me? Really?"

"Truly, I do." I placed a tender kiss on her rosy lips. "I never believed love was possible for me, yet I love you beyond imagining."

"I guess you need to stretch that imagination of yours," she teased, then persuaded me that words were an inadequate expression of my ardor.

Some while later, with the fire burning low in the grate and our own flames momentarily quenched, Rosa resumed her questions concerning our future together.

"Okay, but do you know about this happening to any other djinn? I mean, are you human now? Will you live a normal human lifespan? And, most importantly—" She looped her arms around my neck. "Will you stay with me? I want to be with you for as long as we have, Ardeth. I love you."

"You will have me until the end of our days, my love. That is my wish for us both."

18

ROSA

ONE YEAR LATER

Life is good. Like, really, really good. I can hardly believe it.

My business has taken off to the point where I've hired an assistant to help with booking commissions, managing my schedule, keeping my supplies in stock, taking care of the bookkeeping, and shipping items to their new owners. Of course, the increase in work also meant I had to give up my job at the library. It frees me up to do the part I love. Much more of this, though, and I'll be booked out so far in advance that I may need to take on an apprentice.

Me, Rosa Jenkins, with a real, live apprentice. Who woulda thunk?

Our household is now complete with two rescue cats, Sarina and Moose. Sarina is Ardeth's, and they totally love each other. It's fitting since Ardeth is kind of slinky and sexy, almost feline. I'd wanted a dog, but since Ardeth isn't really a dog person, I got a huge cat who *thinks* he's a dog. Moose is my baby, part Maine Coon (or so I'm told), and he drives Ardeth and Sarina bananas with all his energy. Best of all, he likes to go for walks with us on his leash. Together, we're a happy little family.

To keep himself busy now that he doesn't have any magic whatsoever, and nothing much to do while I'm working, Ardeth has been volunteering at the homeless shelter. He helps with signing people in, doing laundry, and setting up toiletry kits for new arrivals. Sometimes, he even reads stories to the kids. I went to pick him up one day, and I got to hear him read. With that amazing voice of his, he had everyone mesmerized, including me.

Ardeth seems to be actually human in every way we can think of. He's still big and tall, but more in the realm of what you'd actually see in a human man. And he's still endowed exactly as he was when he died. Lucky me! His golden complexion has remained. We haven't decided to test the whole can-he-impregnate-me aspect, though. That will have to remain a mystery for the foreseeable future.

Foreseeable, ha!

And speaking of mysteries, Ardeth doesn't know if this transformation has ever happened before, the whole djinn-turned-human thing. It could be just part of that strange prophecy he told me about. So we still have questions, but they don't matter as long as we're together.

Basically, I've got everything I ever could have hoped for, as well as some things I never would have dreamed were possible.

I couldn't wish for more.

THANK YOU FOR READING!

If you enjoyed *Wish On a Winter Moon*, please leave a review. It helps other readers find it in the vast sea of books in the world.

For the latest news from K. Kiely/Karen Kiely including freebies and book releases, sign up for my newsletter at https://www.karenkielyauthor.com/

AUTHOR NOTE

When I started writing this book featuring a djinn, I had a pretty good idea how it would go, what direction it would take.

I knew nothing, Jon Snow.

It went places I didn't anticipate, and I found the need to take great care in how I incorporated the djinn into my story. I hope I treated my portrayal of the djinn with the respect that is deserved. This is a decidedly Western view shown here, and any missteps and mistakes are all mine, and not at all intentional.

For a list of possible content warnings, please check my website at https://www.karenkielyauthor.com/

ACKNOWLEDGMENTS

I have so many people to thank, and while I hate to admit it, I'm sure I'm forgetting some. My heartfelt apologies to any not named here.

First, thanks to Elizabeth Allyn-Dean, Neva Post and Erin HB for the idea to write a paranormal romance, and giving me a project to break out of my 3+ year long writing stalemate.

The hugest thanks ever to my critique partners, Elizabeth Allyn-Dean, Neva Post, and Kinsley Adams, for the encouragement and criticism to get me through to the end. I couldn't do this without you.

I had the best beta readers in Erin McLellan, Erin HB, and Emily Hemenway. Your perspectives are invaluable to me.

My current and former AKRWA peeps have been a fantastic source of support and knowledge in my writing and publishing journey. Thank you for sharing your wisdom with me.

I've been so fortunate to have friends and family (including my beloved Hags) who cheered me on from the first words of fiction I wrote via NaNoWriMo 2015 until now. Thanks for your encouragement even when I devolve into gibberish and gestures.

And, most especially, thank you to my children, Ian and Katherine. I hope I make you as proud as you make me. Love you always!

ABOUT THE AUTHOR

Karen Kiely (aka K. Kiely) is a lifelong Alaskan who has never had a polar bear for a pet, but if you ask, she'll tell you all about the orphaned black bear cub who came to live with her family for a week. She writes romance in the contemporary and paranormal lanes, filled with sensuality, humor, and recognizable Alaskan details. When she's not writing or talking to her writing friends, she's reading, listening to podcasts, and masquerading as furniture for her cats while catching up on her streaming queue.

You can find her at her website: https://www. karenkielyauthor.com/